Strangers on the 16:02

Priya Basil

BLACK SWAN

TRANSWORLD PUBLISHERS
61–63 Uxbridge Road, London W5 5SA
A Random House Group Company
www.rbooks.co.uk

STRANGERS ON THE 16:02
A BLACK SWAN BOOK: 9780552777056

First publication in Great Britain
Corgi edition published 2011

A CIP catalogue record for this book is available from the British Library.

Addresses for Random House Group Ltd companies outside the UK can be found at: www.randomhouse.co.uk
The Random House Group Reg. No. 954009

The Random House Group Limited supports The Forest Stewardship Council (FSC), the leading international forest certification organization. All our titles that are printed on Greenpeace approved FSC certified paper carry the FSC logo. Our paper procurement policy can be found at www.rbooks.co.uk/environment

Typeset in 12/16pt Stone Serif by
Kestrel Data, Exeter, Devon.
Printed in the UK by
CPI Cox & Wyman, Reading, RG1 8EX.

2 4 6 8 10 9 7 5 3

Priya Basil was born in London and grew up in [illegible] and Berlin and [illegible]

Visit her at www.Priyabasil.com

www.quickreads.org.uk

www.rbooks.co.uk

Also by Priya Basil

Ishq and Mushq
The Obscure Logic of the Heart

and published by Black Swan

To my brother Agam, who related an incident that inspired this story

Thanks to my ever-wonderful editor Jane Lawson. I'm also grateful to all the different people at Transworld Publishers and Quick Reads who helped in various ways with this book. Thanks as well to the team at my agency Rogers, Coleridge & White.

Strangers on the 16:02

Chapter One

Helen is wishing it was all out in the open. Then she wouldn't have to pretend.

Helen Summers re-reads the words she's typed into her mobile phone. Just one more tap on the screen and the two sentences will be posted, through the internet link in her phone, onto her Facebook page. All her Facebook friends will be able to see the comment. There's a chance Jill, her sister, might spot it too. Helen's index finger remains in mid-air, unsure whether to press down and seal her fate.

The train she's on suddenly swerves around a bend, and she grabs at the nearby rail to steady herself. Outside, the terraced houses, open playing fields and dowdy high streets of London's outer suburbs slip by under a darkening winter sky.

A strange mix of commuters surrounds Helen. They're not the suited crowd who fill the carriages at peak times, their faces grey with the stress of long journeys between work and home.

This 16:02 train from Hampton to Waterloo is carrying a different kind of traveller. The sort who by chance, design, bad luck or, like Helen, due to some mishap, has escaped, for today at least, the humdrum nine-to-five routine. There are senior citizens with Freedom Passes, cleaners heading for offices that will soon be empty and tourists fresh from seeing Tudor history at Hampton Court Palace.

Helen's hazel eyes remain fixed on her phone. The gadget is also connected to her ears, with music travelling up a white cord to some earphones. She lets go of the handrail and moves her feet further apart so she can balance better. Then she takes a deep breath and posts the comment on her Facebook page.

There, it's done. A sigh of relief and a jolt of worry pass through her at the same time. She thinks of the man whose actions have put her in this mess. Just the hint of his face in her mind's eye makes her shiver. She had never trusted Danny. His Aston Martin and designer clothes didn't persuade her that his online business, selling land in space, was a success.

OK, all this climate change end-of-the-world stuff was getting serious. And yes, a few people who weren't astronauts, but were rich enough, had travelled to outer space, but still. Helen couldn't believe there were many people ready to pay money for a piece of paper that claimed they owned a plot of land somewhere that wasn't on earth.

Was it even legal? Helen had often wondered. Didn't you have to own something to sell it? What right did Danny have to flog off bits of the solar system for his own profit? Then again, as Helen's mother, Sheila, liked to say, 'That man would sell water to the sea if he had half a chance.'

Helen shakes her head. Why is she focusing on him? She raises the volume of the music so the sound blots out her thoughts. Already replies to her Facebook post are starting to appear. She reads them:

Carrie Marsh: Sounds scary. What's going on?
David Grimleigh: R u OK?
Pablo Perez: Heh? Good or bad?

Helen smiles at her phone. This concern has the same effect as a hand stroking her back and makes her feel less alone. Another post pops up:

Parveen Oberoi: Are you pregnant?

That makes her laugh out loud. One or two people turn to look. The eyes of the man sitting in front of Helen flick up. He looks for the source of the lively giggle. A sound that cuts through the quiet of the carriage like the trill of an exotic bird piercing the silence of a graveyard.

The man sees plump, but shapely calves rising out of some ankle boots. Fuck-me shoes, that's what his friends call this kind of footwear, and for the first time Kerm understands what they mean. The long, thin, spiky heels make his lips pucker, as if he's about to whistle. His right leg is almost between hers; if he stretched out and lifted it up . . .

He whips his head round, looking over one shoulder as if there's something he can't miss outside the window. Control yourself, man, he tells himself. It seems especially wrong to be having such thoughts today, just hours after his grandfather's funeral.

Through his work he has grown used to death. He doesn't see it as often as he did when he was a junior doctor training in hospital, but he gets a hint of it almost every day. Usually it's via his older patients, but sometimes they are young, even younger than him, and often they seem healthier than him too. These are the cases that shake him up and make him vow to give up smoking. Until two hours later, when he finds himself ducking around the back of the surgery for a cigarette.

Baoji was the first person close to Kerm who has died, though the closeness was more of blood than of the heart. Kerm's deeper feelings lie with his mother's side of the family, but his fate, if the elders are to be believed, is bound up with his father's side of the family. They were men remembered for their authority and long lives.

Kerm was born exactly one hundred and one years (to the day) after his great-grandfather on his father's side, Kamaveer Singh Vora. This was seen as a good sign because Sikhs consider odd numbers to be especially lucky. With gifts of money, for example, they never give a whole number. One extra pound is always added to the sum, so, for example, it's £21, £51, £101 . . .

Some of Kerm's father's relatives are convinced that he is the reincarnation of his great-grandfather. The older female members of the Vora family often say, 'Niri Veer-ji', meaning 'the spitting image of Veer'. They pat Kerm's high cheekbones, pull at his long chin, tap his sharp nose and shake their heads at the likeness.

His face may display the typical Vora features,

but Kerm's physique comes from his mother. The Vora men tend to be short and stocky, while Kerm is tall and gangly. That's why he was nicknamed Kermit, later shortened by almost everyone to Kerm.

Sometimes he wonders jokingly who he is. Where is Kerm in this being whose soul is said to come from an ancestor and whose body is not completely his own either?

Kerm has had trouble with his eyesight and has had to have both eyes operated on. His left cornea – the see-through disc at the front of the eyeball – once belonged to a nineteen-year-old from Glasgow who died of a stab wound to the heart. His right cornea was donated by a fifty-one-year-old German woman who died of a stroke.

Try as he might, Kerm can't forget about this. As a doctor, he understands the science of transplants. He's aware that corneas don't age or change unless there is some specific direct damage, like an acid burn. So there's no chance that the lives of his donors have affected their corneas. Moreover, Kerm knows that just because you have someone else's heart or eyes, doesn't mean you start feeling or seeing like them.

And yet, there's a part of him that believes some experiences can invade the blood, flesh, organs and even the cells of people. He himself has been, and is still being, formed and changed in this way. He doesn't want to remember some of the things, but they are embedded in him. They are a kind of DNA that affects everything, and they're all the more powerful for being unseen.

Chapter Two

Kerm had last visited his grandfather in hospital two days before his death. He knew that in his family's opinion he hadn't gone often enough. He'd made it three times during the five weeks Baoji had been an in-patient. It would have felt false to turn up more regularly. A closeness that had never existed couldn't suddenly be forced, Kerm felt.

'You don't go just for the one who's dying,' his mother had said, 'you go to support those who will be most affected by the loss, like your father. Go for your dad's sake, Kerm.' Her logic would have made sense if the bond with his father had been stronger. Sadly, it too was flimsy, like a rope weakened by neglect rather than over-use.

Nevertheless Kerm had gone, maybe because showing up at such moments was one of the basic principles of being a family. And also because having your father's approval still seemed to matter, even when you were thirty-two years old, and already owned a better car than any your father had driven.

The first time Kerm had been to the hospital was two weeks before the end, on a Saturday afternoon. He'd caught a whiff of curry as he got out of the lift in the Medicine for the Elderly unit. He assumed the hospital had served Indian food for lunch that day, but in his grandfather's ward the smell was much stronger. It was as if an Indian fair was in full swing.

Baoji's four sons and one daughter were there, and everyone except Kerm's dad had a spouse with them. Some had brought children and grandchildren along, too. Even Sam, the son who hadn't spoken to his father for years, had come over from Uganda. Everyone was crowded around the bed, chatting, snacking and arguing as if they were at home. Kerm couldn't believe the hospital had allowed such a crowd, let alone such a smell, to build up.

While his Aunt Veena offered him samosas, Kerm glanced at the other patients in the ward, and beyond them towards the nurses' station.

'Don't worry, Dr Kermit, I've given them some as well. I haven't been coming here all these weeks without learning a thing or two.' Veena took a bite of the samosa Kerm had refused.

'All these weeks!' Her brother Vishal said as he ushered Kerm through the ring of bodies towards Baoji. 'You were in Canada when Dad was admitted. You only got back ten days ago.'

'Well, I've been here morning to night ever since, unlike some people who have to go to work.' Veena stood with one hand on her hip, while the other held her half-eaten samosa in mid-air. 'It's been a full-time job for me. Feels like longer than ten days.'

The other uncles and aunts began welcoming Kerm. His Aunt Sajini piped up with her usual, 'Hello, Kermit, how's your mummy?' Her eyes were always on Kerm's dad as she asked the question, as though she expected him to burst into tears, even twenty years after the divorce.

Baoji was a picture of peace amidst his loud family. Maybe there were some advantages to having poor sight and hearing in old age, Kerm thought. The old man looked so small. It was hard to believe those narrow, bony shoulders poking through the green hospital vest were the same ones Kerm had climbed on as a child.

'He looks all right, doesn't he?' one of the uncles said.

Kerm swallowed. He knew how easy it was to get used to illness, how even the most wasted face could begin to look normal to those who saw it every day. Maybe Baoji had been worse before. Perhaps he was looking better compared to last week. 'Is he showing signs of improvement then?'

'Yah yah. You know he ate quite well today.' Kerm's dad, Rajan, pointed to the plastic bottle on Baoji's bedside table. It looked like the kind of thing body builders might drink to bulk up on muscle. In fact it was an orange-coloured liquid rich in nutrients that was given to patients who could no longer eat properly. 'I managed to get three spoons of that down him this morning.'

'Well, I managed to feed him five spoons last night,' Veena added. In her brightly patterned outfit, she looked like one of the flower arrangements on the nearby shelf. 'That sounds good, doesn't it, Kerm?'

He nodded slowly. It didn't seem the moment to suggest otherwise.

A nurse came up then to say there were too many people around the hospital bed. 'I'm afraid it's a fire hazard,' she said, screwing up her nose as if the smoke had already got to her. 'Only six at a time maximum. The rest of you will have to wait outside and take it in turns.'

'But he's a doctor,' Veena pointed at Kerm.

The nurse raised her eyebrows as if she didn't see the point of the comment.

'Anyway, nurse,' Veena crossed her arms under her heavy breasts, 'my father's sheets haven't been changed today, and we're still waiting for the consultant. My nephew', she pointed at Kerm again, 'has some professional queries for him.'

Kerm winced. Offers of smelly food, veiled threats and bragging about the doctors amongst your visitors was not the way to get hospital staff on side. They were exactly the type of family he and his fellow doctors had joked about when he had done his training. They were the kind of people nobody wanted to treat. The kind you tossed a coin for and cursed when you lost.

Chapter Three

As the train approaches a station, Kerm can see the platforms heaving with people, many of them dressed the same way. He's about to get caught in the end-of-school rush. He turns away from the window again, unfolds the newspaper lying in his lap and tries to read, but soon his eyes stray back to the woman with the lovely laugh.

Kerm's gaze follows the length of the camel-coloured suede coat that drapes three-quarters of her body. The flowing cut of the garment shows little of her figure. There's a splash of emerald-green wool where the buttons of the coat are open at her chest. A thin gold chain glistens against the pale skin at her throat. She has a pretty face: her slightly chubby cheeks look healthy and her skin is as smooth and flawless as a child's. Her eyes are cast down, fixed on the screen of her phone, but he can see long black lashes curving upwards.

The train doors open and an insanity of noise hits Kerm's ears. It's so loud they could be passing through a zoo where a premiership football match is taking place. School children pile onto the train in groups, jostling one another and talking noisily. Some are in uniform, ties askew, blazers hanging off one shoulder. Others take casual-wear to absurd extremes: guys in jeans with waistbands sagging below the bum, and girls defying the winter weather by flashing bare legs under their skirts. Nearly all the students hold carrier bags marked with a sports brand logo. The sharp corners of files or text books poke through the plastic, jabbing into anyone close by.

Helen, who's still standing in the middle of the carriage, between two rows of seats, has hardly noticed the crowd thickening around her. The mini speakers tucked into her ears ooze an electronic funk that masks the noise of the train and other passengers. Helen's eyes remain glued to her phone. Her cheeks are covered by shoulder-length brown hair that falls forwards, cutting off the view on either side. She scrolls down her Facebook page, enjoying the messages posted by friends:

Tina just ate a 6-serving chocolate pudding to get her through the chaos. It helped.

Helen taps on the option 'Like' that appears just below the comment, and her name is added to the tally of five other people to have given Tina's comment a thumbs-up. She does the same for another remark Tina posted that afternoon, an hour after the first one:

Tina wants to know when her hips will finally give way to her will.

All Tina's Facebook chat is somehow related to her weight. Helen can sympathise because she too is on a constant crusade against calories. She smiles as she reads John Manfield's update:

John knows that no one looks back at their life and remembers the nights they got plenty of sleep.

Sometimes, Helen feels, there is more practical wisdom to be found on Facebook than in the philosophical texts she studies at university. Occasionally, she finds, Facebook is even more entertaining than a good novel. There's a lot more room for playing guessing games because you know the characters personally and the plot can have countless strands. What's more, you can chip in with a line or two of your own and maybe even influence the outcome. Facebook as the future of fiction: maybe that should be the subject of her next essay. She giggles aloud as she reads another update:

Janet caught Jessie's vomit in her cupped hands in the middle of Tesco food hall this lunchtime.

Helen continues to scroll down the screen, enjoying other people's mistakes and musings. Then she sees another comment appear in response to her own post. It's from Jeremy Turner:

'Where (or of what) one cannot speak, one must pass over in silence.'

Helen comes out in goose bumps. She can almost feel the hairs on her arms stiffen and prick against her clothes. Jeremy is one of her tutors, the youngest professor in a department where no one is under forty. He's an expert on the philosopher Wittgenstein and a regular user of Facebook. Most of his activity on the social network involves him posting profound quotations that are spookily relevant to most daily situations.

No doubt her mum would approve of that quote, Helen thinks. It is Sheila who has sworn her daughter to silence for the next ten days. As

Helen remembers their conversation a few hours earlier she feels anger pump through her body. At the same time guilt trickles through her, drip, drip, drip, as if there's a leak inside, some hole in her mental and emotional armour that can't be fixed. It's all Danny's fault, she thinks. If it wasn't for him . . .

Helen's fingers expertly work the keys on the touch-screen of the phone cradled between her palms, composing . . . what? A confession? An apology? A brief statement of the facts? Whatever she writes, she's going to end up doing exactly what her mother has begged her not to: she's going to tell her sister, Jill, the truth.

Helen mistypes a couple of times as passengers nudge past, pushing against her. At one point she almost loses her balance and looks up, her eyes narrowing in irritation. She sees that the carriage is packed with school kids and that she's squashed between them. Some man's knee is also pressed against her inner calf. She quickly moves her leg, as if by distancing herself from this man she can set herself apart from the whole male species. Danny's actions have put Helen off all men. She's sure she can never be attracted to anyone of the opposite sex again. Helen bends slightly and squints out of the window, trying to see which station they're at.

No sign is visible, but she recognises the lamp posts: the distinctive tall poles with two lights perched on top, like the wings of a giant wasp. It's Twickenham. The very stop she herself commuted to and from as a sixth-former at college. It was only five years ago, the last time she boarded the train here, but already it feels like another era. She can't imagine herself as one of the rowdy creatures that now swarm the carriage. Actually, she never was one of them. She'd been too clever, too fat and too shy to fit in with her peers.

They're all around her now, though, elbows in her side, trainers scuffing against her boots, their mouths moving in conversations from which she's excluded. Today it's by choice, thanks to the music coming through her headphones, but in the past . . . She's surprised to feel a familiar mixture of fear mingled with longing and disdain, the unpleasant cocktail of her teenage years.

Usually, when she's heading back towards West London from her mother's place, Helen is careful to take one of the trains that go via a different route. Today, however, a train had been on the platform when she'd arrived at the station and she'd rushed on it to get away from Sheila and her scheming.

Chapter Four

The police had contacted Helen by phone earlier that afternoon while she'd been at her parents' place. She and her mum had been in the shed at the bottom of their long garden. The little wooden shack, which sat under the old walnut tree, had become a dumping ground for items that were no longer wanted by the family, but were still useable. There they lived in the dusty gloom for a few months until Sheila held one of her car boot sales, and whatever wasn't sold went to charity. Sheila found comfort in this regular clear-out, especially as it gave her a good excuse to buy new things.

One such boot sale was planned for the coming Sunday. Helen had gone home to have a final rummage through the shed and see if there was anything she wanted; at least that's what she'd told her mum. She was actually keen to make sure none of her stuff was amongst the goods to be sold. Sheila had a habit of putting anything she thought her daughters no longer used in the shed, ready for the next sale or for charity. Last year, Helen's entire summer wardrobe had been lost this way. She'd stored the clothes in two boxes and left them in the corner of her old room during winter, because there wasn't much space at the flat she lived in. Her mother had thought she didn't want them any more and promptly sold them in a car boot sale.

Just as well Helen had come by this afternoon, because within minutes of entering the shed she'd spotted something that shouldn't have been there.

'Mum! Why is this here?' Helen pulled her suede coat out from under a pile of clothes. The single bare bulb glared brightly above them, throwing funny shadows onto the walls.

Sheila lifted her glasses from the bridge of her nose and peered under them to look at the garment Helen was thrusting in her face. 'It's been hanging on the back of your bedroom door for years now, dear. I thought you didn't wear it any more.'

'Well, that doesn't mean I'll never want to!' In fact, Helen had an urge to put the coat on right away. She'd forgotten how nice it was. Her fingers brushed at the soft, sand-coloured fabric. 'I've told you before, don't just take stuff without asking me first.' She draped the coat over her forearm. 'I love this coat.' It was definitely going back home with her today.

'Yes, but really, how am I supposed to . . . Helen! Do you have to get that now?' Sheila sighed as Helen reached into the pocket of her skirt for her phone. Its ringing sounded like a horn in the small space of the shed. 'You're addicted to that thing. Really!' She would have gone on complaining, only she saw Helen's face change.

First she went pale, then her skin flushed a deep pink. 'Yes, yes, this is Helen Summers,' she said. She turned her back on her mother as the conversation continued.

It was Police Constable Ted Priestly from the Hammersmith and Fulham police station. The officer informed her that they had the results of their investigation into the identity of the mystery-caller who'd been harassing her for the last six months. Helen's instinct was to hold the phone away from her ear as part of her didn't want to know who the culprit might be.

To begin with, the calls had been infrequent, once every couple of weeks. Usually the person rang just after midnight. No number showed up on the screen of Helen's phone, just the word 'Withheld'. All she could hear when she answered was heavy breathing. The first couple of times she imagined that her number had been dialled by accident, so she'd hung up after saying 'Hello?' several times. Then the guy had started talking, trying to keep her on the phone a few seconds longer. His voice was strange, extra deep and with an accent that could have been American. One time he'd said, 'I'm coming,' and she'd answered, 'Where?' She'd looked around the flat, expecting someone to break in, until she heard the grunts coming through the receiver. She'd slammed down the phone and decided to report the incidents.

'We've traced the number and identity of the caller,' the officer said.

Helen felt the blood pounding at her temples. She sensed her mother move closer behind her.

'Do you know of a man called Daniel Peel?' he went on.

The coat slipped off Helen's arm onto the floor. She turned around with her eyes shut tight and shoved the phone at her mother. She pushed against one wall to steady herself, and then, feeling her way along it, moved slowly towards the door. Outside, she doubled over, clutching her stomach. Her mother's voice drifted out of the shed, loud with shock, then louder with anger.

'Why didn't you tell me, dear?' Sheila hurried out to her daughter and held Helen, stroking her hair and rubbing her back. 'What a vile piece of work that man is. Oh, your poor sister. Why didn't you tell me?'

'I didn't know it was him!'

'But that this was happening at all! You never said. Oh God, what are we going to do? Your sister . . .' Sheila started leading Helen back towards the house, the damp grass squeaking under their feet. Both of them went through the back door wearing their wet wellingtons.

Helen's dad, Peter, was sitting on the sofa in the living room. His feet, clad in woollen house shoes, were perched on a side table that had been pulled up for just that purpose, while a pipe was secured to his lips. Under the collar of his check shirt, a red scarf was wrapped around his neck as a permanent defence against the cold he was always 'just about to get'. He looked up from his newspaper as the women walked across the carpet, his eyes following the muddy trail of footprints they were leaving on its light blue surface.

Sheila's eyebrows did a coded dance for her husband as she made Helen sit down next to him on the brown leather sofa. Peter lifted his feet off the table, put the paper to one side and began puffing on his pipe with energy.

Helen's eyes were squeezed shut but still the

tears leaked silently out of them. Some had travelled all the way down her face and neck, trickling under the round neckline of her green mohair sweater. She took hold of the tissues that her mum was rubbing against her cheeks.

Over her head Sheila gave Peter a quick whispered rundown of what the police officer had said. Quite what the low volume and speed of speech were supposed to achieve, Helen had no idea. They could have talked normally. It wasn't like she didn't know what was going on. She heard the light 'clack' of her father's pipe being set down and the sound made her realise how awful the discovery of the caller's identity was. Anything, apart from basic daily necessities, that prompted Peter to stop smoking and put down his pipe was serious.

The name 'Jill' popped out of Sheila's mouth with a frequency that seemed odd to Helen. From the way her mother talked you'd think something terrible had happened to Helen's sister while her own experience was only minor. Of course, Helen realised, the implications probably were more serious for Jill, but this over-the-top concern was typical of her parents. They had always treated weedy, asthmatic Jill like a fragile flower, while plump, chirpy Helen was assumed to be the tough one.

'So I don't know. I just don't know.' Sheila's palms spread out. 'How is Jill going to take this?'

Helen's eyes sprang open. The room appeared unnaturally fuzzy and bright. Slowly, it came back into focus again. She was surprised to find the world looking the same rather than washed over with the sickly yellow of her feelings.

'Why is this just about her?' Helen blurted out.

Peter cleared his throat and patted his daughter's knee. His hand was tense, the fingers stiff, so that they felt like a piece of board tapping against Helen. Her father was not good at displaying affection.

'Well, Danny *is* her husband.' Sheila gave her spouse a sideways look, as if their daughter had gone mad.

'Yes, but it's me he's done something to. Me!' Helen's fingers jabbed against her chest. 'No one seems to be bothered about that.'

'He's behaved disgustingly. There's no question about it.' The pressure of Peter's hand on Helen's kneecap increased.

'Well, of course. You poor dear.' Sheila came over and squatted before her husband and daughter, pulling them both into a group hug.

'It's just awful, but at least it's over for you now, whereas Jill—'

'Over?' Helen shot off the sofa so fast her father's hand was thrown in the air and her mother almost fell backwards. She paced the room, her hands clenched into fists. On the wall behind her was a collage of photos. The moments – birthdays, weddings, graduations – captured in those pictures were supposed to represent all the important events in the family's life, but they rarely captured the real dramas. The times that ended up mattering most were ones like this, where no one would even think of taking a photo.

'How is it over?' Helen repeated. As she stared at her mother, Helen's bottom lip peeled away from the top one and her mouth hung open. Just because the identity of the caller was known, it didn't mean the whole experience was done and dusted for her. In fact, the awfulness of it was just beginning to hit Helen. The idea of Danny calling and putting on that voice while Jill was probably asleep in the next room . . .

She swung round and riffled her hands through her pockets. 'Where's my phone? I want to call that man now!'

Both her parents started speaking at once.

'Let's not be rash about this.' Her father tried

to get her to sit down again, but Helen refused. 'Come on.' He took hold of her wrists, gently forcing her to stand still and pay attention.

'You have to consider how many other people are involved—' Sheila started, but stopped when she saw Peter's grey eyes narrow.

'Now,' he began, slowly and logically, to run through the facts, 'Danny has wronged you. There's police evidence for this. You have the right to press charges. He's also Jill's husband. She loves him—'

'She doesn't know better!' Sheila interrupted.

'Whatever we might think of the man, she does love him,' Peter insisted, his eyes still on Helen.

'Or she thinks she does,' Sheila muttered. Then she pressed her lips together and dug her hands into the pockets of her long cardigan. She looked down and noticed all the mud on the carpet. A huge sigh heaved out of her, like a toilet being flushed.

'So, Helen, you need to be careful about how you tell Jill,' Peter went on. 'She may be against you taking legal action—'

'That's not my pr—' Helen started, but Peter cut her short.

'I'm not saying that she'd be right, you just need to be aware of this so you can decide how to deal with it.' He had all the options and possibilities lined up in his head, like a long equation full of brackets, plus and equals signs. A life of teaching maths had left him with a tendency to filter all problems in this way, turning them into sums to which solutions might be found at some stage. He went on listing things and the steadiness of his deep voice was calming for Helen. Being a rational person herself, she understood the sense of his words, even though a huge part of her wanted Danny punished right away.

'And you know,' Sheila jumped in as soon as Peter was finished, 'we've got to use this chance!' She said it as if it was a gift. For several years Sheila had been fretting over how she could separate Jill from Danny. Now, Helen could see a brightness that verged on excitement in her mother's anger. She was ready to turn a disaster into an opportunity.

'You're happy.' Helen moved out of her father's grip and faced her mum.

'What? Don't be—'

'You're glad you finally have something against Danny that you can use to save poor, helpless Jill.' Helen crossed her arms over her chest. 'It doesn't matter about me.'

'That's not true!' Tears jabbed at the inner corners of Sheila's eyes.

'You're not being fair, Helen.' Peter took a few steps so he was standing by his wife's side.

'I hate him for what he's done to both of you.' Sheila pulled Helen into her arms again.

'We must have the policeman there when we tell Jill, otherwise she won't believe us!' Sheila's neat, short eyebrows bounced over the lenses of her rimless glasses. 'You know how she is when it comes to Danny.'

Helen did indeed. That was one point she couldn't argue with.

'That man could convince her that Eskimos live on the beach. If he gets a chance to speak to her before we do, he'll twist everything . . .' Sheila stepped back and her eyes swung from her husband to Helen. 'I wouldn't put it past him to make out that Helen . . .' She left the idea hanging.

It was really the truth of this fact that had brought Helen round to her parents' way of doing things, because she knew just how devious Danny could be.

'There's only one way to handle him,' Sheila had said, and she knew exactly what that was.

Chapter Five

Back in the train, as she recalls the afternoon's events, Helen feels frustrated at being forced into following her parents' advice. Their plan is for a big post-party showdown with Danny and PC Priestly present. Sheila was determined that nothing should spoil the party she had spent two months planning for Jill's birthday. The way she'd gone on about how much Jill was looking forward to it, you'd have thought Jill was turning three, not thirty.

For Helen, the thought of sitting tight and pretending nothing has happened for more than a week seems unbearable. It might just be possible if she doesn't get another call from Danny in that time, but then there is the fact that she will have to go to the party and pretend for the whole evening while that monster of a man is right there. No doubt he'll ham up the devotion, play the perfect husband and give some speech about true love. The corners of Helen's mouth pull down in disgust.

No, she decides, she's not going to keep quiet.

She stares at her phone and the half-written message she's composed. Why put off the inevitable just for the sake of a party? The truth was going to ruin Jill's life for a while anyway. Or maybe it wouldn't. Maybe Jill would continue to believe that Danny was the man of her dreams.

Jill had an uncanny ability to put a positive spin on everything her husband did. Last year she'd suspected him of having an affair. She'd confronted him about it after a wedding reception at which the woman in question had repeatedly drawn Danny aside in order to have her picture taken with him. Danny had responded to Jill's questions by hitting her.

'He was really hurt,' Jill told her sister a few days later when Helen had popped over to see her. 'He was so upset that I could think him capable of such a thing. That's why he slapped me.' Her hand unconsciously rubbed the left jaw where his blow had landed and there was still the faint blue hint of a bruise. 'Now I know how much he loves me.'

'What? I don't see how violence can ever be interpreted as love!' Helen set her mug down roughly causing tea to slop over the side onto the stainless-steel kitchen counter. She couldn't tell how much Jill's words were the result of brain-washing by Danny or her sister's wilful blindness. 'He's no good for you! You could do a million times better.'

'But I love him,' was Jill's pitiful refrain, the same as it had been for the last six years.

Love! There were times when Helen felt the word was a curse, something to be avoided, not aspired to.

'You don't understand.' Jill lifted her sister's mug. She wiped it and the counter with a dish-cloth, then she tried to polish away some of the smudges Helen's fingers had left on the other-wise perfectly shiny surface. The sun poured in from the skylight overhead and bounced off the metal counters.

'I feel so bad for thinking that of him. It was completely wrong of me.' Jill shook her head. Her copper-coloured fringe brushed along her eyebrows.

Helen was speechless for a while. Her mouth opened and closed a few times as if she was warming up her jaw for some exercise. 'How was it wrong?' she eventually said. 'Your doubts didn't come out of nowhere.'

'Danny says it's my own insecurity that makes me suspicious.' Jill shrugged her thin shoulders as though there was no room for argument.

Her sister's marriage was the most twisted

example of human weakness parading as love that Helen had ever seen. It was even worse than the strange relationship between her parents. Helen had broken the family mould in so far as she had never let herself be manipulated by a man, for good or bad. As a result, her mother liked to point out, she had made herself a victim of her own high standards. 'What's the fun in standing on the outskirts of love and feeling superior?' Sheila had once asked. 'There's no shame in having got it wrong. Whereas it's a shame when you don't even give yourself the chance of getting it right. Better to have loved and lost . . .'

Helen is twenty-three years old and has never had a boyfriend. No man has impressed or reassured her enough. There have been only drunken propositions, or friendships that teetered on the brink of something more for so long they fizzled back into friendship.

On the train, bodies press in on Helen from all sides. She inches towards the row of seated passengers, trying to create a fraction of space between herself and the rest of the crowd, but it makes no difference. The knees of the man sitting in front are pressing into her legs again. Someone else's bum is rubbing against her hip.

Her right shoulder is pinned to the ample bosom of a young girl with two piercings in each eyebrow and, as far as Helen can tell, more students are still piling onto the train.

All this brazen body contact makes her feel queasy. She doesn't know why, but the expression 'sexual congress' pops into her head. Maybe it has something to do with the notion of people gathering together implied by 'congress' and the idea of them all packed together in a way that suggests intimacy.

There is something rather sexual about all these mingled limbs, rubbing clothes and the inhalation of other people's breath and body odour. Or maybe Helen just thinks that because she has so little experience in that regard. The subject always makes her feel a little prim. Even in her mind her vocabulary changes, and words related to sex are expressed with a special emphasis, as though she's dealing with something very delicate.

She's not aware of it, but her posture has altered too. She's standing stiff and upright, her chin jutting upwards as though the carriage has filled with water reaching the top of her neck. Helen leans back so she isn't lodged right under the upraised arm of the man standing next to her. He smells of wet cat, like a lot of people who wear those quilted, country-style jackets . . .

The train restarts with a few jerks, as if it's struggling to cope with the extra load it has just picked up. After a moment, it eases smoothly along the tracks and starts gliding through the darkness.

Helen finishes typing the message to Jill*: We need 2 talk ASAP. About D.* Her finger hovers over the 'send' button for a few seconds, then she presses 'save'. Perhaps she should send it later, once she's home. It wouldn't be ideal if Jill called back right now.

Her lips part in amusement as she flicks back to her Facebook page.

Tina is brownie mad (that's the food, not the institution).

How much time and thought can a person devote to food? A lot. Helen should know. Now that she eats less she seems to dream even more about food. One meal is hardly over and she's looking forward to the next. At any given moment she can list what her meals over the coming twenty-four hours will be. Dinner tonight: grilled salmon with steamed broccoli and brown rice, followed by the leftover pear crumble from yesterday. This reminds her that she needs to buy some cream on the way home. One of her flatmates had used up what was left in the pot for his coffee this morning because there was no more milk. The trials of flat sharing.

Helen can't wait until she has her own place. Everything would finally be just the way she wants it: the toilet roll would hang the right way in its holder and the jam wouldn't be filled with crumbs and blobs of butter from people dipping dirty knives into the jar. The TV wouldn't be on even when no one was watching it; wet bath towels wouldn't be left hanging on the back of the sofa. The thought of what she has to put up with makes Helen shudder. If it wasn't for her the flat in Baron's Court would be a tip, and yet her fellow students complain that she's the one who's difficult to live with.

Chapter Six

Two carriages down, right at the back of the train, Innocent Babatunde and his two friends, Blessing and Comfort, are playing tunes to each other from their mobiles. No earpieces for them. They use their phones like mini-stereos, blasting out music so that everyone can hear. The volume is up so high that every word of their rap songs is audible, even above the lively chatter of their fellow passengers.

'Awww, this is one sick tune.' Innocent sucks his cheeks against his teeth. 'These bars are greeze, blud. I need a copy.' Even though he's pleased, his face doesn't show it. There's a surly set to his mouth, as though he's permanently pissed off with the world.

Approval for the music comes from his fellow students. Their high fives are loaded with a respect that has more behind it than a shared taste in music. The three teenagers with the old-fashioned charitable names form a group no one cares to mess with. Well-known for their courage and recklessness, these boys have been dubbed the Unholy Trinity. To many of their peers, they are as invincible as the spiritual trio they're named after. So it follows that the people they diss deserve it, the laws they break are stupid and whatever they're into is cool.

On the train right now, it's tough luck for anyone who doesn't like gangster rap. Only one person dares to complain. An elderly man in a tweed jacket asks, 'Would you mind turning that down, please?'

He's rewarded with a collective stare of contempt.

'Huh?' Blessing raises his eyebrows and lets his mouth drop open. With his chubby cheeks and small, snub nose, he's the one who looks sweet and innocent. His two buddies are taller and tougher.

'We don't all have to listen to that, do we?' The man points at the phone that Blessing is holding up. 'I'm not sure the music is to everybody's taste, and we are in a public space.' The man glances around, hoping to catch a sympathetic eye, but every other adult seems to be absorbed in reading their palms.

'What?' Blessing's features suggest a total lack of understanding. His eyes grow small, his forehead creases. His black skin seems smooth and shiny enough to reflect back any disapproval that comes his way.

'Maybe you could just turn it down a bit?' The man tries again, but already there's a hint of defeat in his voice.

'Ah?' This time Blessing crosses his eyes and shakes his head. It's as if he's been confronted with complete insanity and the only possible response is madness. His friends laugh and turn the volume up even higher.

The music fans fall under the command of the thumping bass. The beat makes their necks and shoulders snake back and forth. A couple of them close their eyes and sway as if they're in a club. The rhythm of the train fits in nicely with the music; its motion is like an extension of theirs.

'Oh-oh, Centi, blud.' Comfort nudges Innocent and points a thumb over his shoulder. A ticket inspector is coming. He's only a metre away, moving slowly through the crowd in his navy-blue uniform.

Innocent rolls his eyes. He glances from the inspector to the door up ahead, which leads to the next carriage. He could probably lose the inspector if he hurries off through the crowd now. The fact that the carriage is so packed would work to his advantage. He'd have to slip off at the next stop and get another train home, but that's not convenient. He wants to go to Blessing's house with the others. He'll just have to buy a ticket.

He busies himself with his phone while those around him present their tickets. When he feels the inspector's eye on him he doesn't look up. His shaved, domed head remains bent in defiance against authority.

'Your ticket, please?' Timothy Odolo asks. The inspector hates all checks that involve being on the train during the post-school rush hour. Nobody gives him more stick than these youngsters. He's devised strategies to deal with them, but they still scare him. They seem to have got cockier over the years, and he gets more hassle now than ever before.

'Yeah, I need a single to East Croydon,' Innocent says. He keeps his eyes on his phone. His fingers move over the keys as though there's something much more important he needs to be getting on with.

A fine is really in order, but Timothy knows what will happen if he gives one to this type of kid. There will be outrage and arguments, then the friends will join in and he'll probably end up calling the police. He doesn't have the stamina for that today. He reaches for the ticket machine hanging from a strap that loops over his left shoulder down to his right hip. He punches in the ticket type and route and then requests the fare.

'That's full price.' Innocent finally looks at the inspector. The man is short and a little tubby. He has a scar on his forehead that disappears under the thick fuzz of his Afro hair. 'I'm a student. I need my discount.'

Timothy takes a deep breath. 'Where's your student railcard?' He prepares to change the ticket, jabbing at the square black buttons on his grey machine.

'I don't have it with me today.' Innocent's chin rises as he speaks. It bears the straggly first traces of the goatee beard he's started to grow. In fact, his railcard ran out a week ago. He hasn't got round to renewing it because the money his mum gave him for the card got spent honouring a bet he'd lost. He has a habit of making impulsive wagers about things he's absolutely sure of, and half the time he turns out to be wrong.

The inspector pauses and takes stock of this kid whose attitude rises off him like steam. There's no way he's going to avoid a fine *and* get the lower priced ticket. 'It's the full fare then. Three pounds.'

'But I'm a student! You know it. I'm here with

all my boyz.' Just an abrupt move of his head and Innocent has several guys speaking up and vouching for him.

'He's one of us, man,' Comfort says.

'We all just come out of college,' another guy adds.

Timothy shrugs. 'If you don't have proof, I have to charge you the full fare.' He notices that Innocent, unlike the other boys, is not carrying any kind of bag holding books. The kid probably thinks he's too cool for that. Timothy guesses, a little unfairly, that he attends school only to collect the weekly £30 incentive that the government pays sixteen- to eighteen-year-olds for full attendance.

'But I do got proof!' Innocent's gaze sweeps over those standing around him. 'You saying my boyz are lying?'

Six pairs of eyes drill into the inspector. Each hard, shining stare feels as piercing as a whistle. Timothy's body stiffens as he tries to resist the pressure being put on him.

'I need official proof.' He reckons the boy is probably telling the truth, but that's not good enough. That's not how the law works.

'Aw, get a life. Why you being so sad? Look at this guy?' Innocent jabs a hand towards the inspector. 'Go do something more worthwhile!'

The gang around him burst into over-loud laughter.

'Three pounds, please.' Timothy taps a finger against his machine. He has a feeling this could go on for ever.

'What's wrong with you? I told you I'm a student and I'm not paying more just because you think I'm not.' Innocent fishes into the back pocket of his jeans for the money he's prepared to pay. He holds out a two-pound coin between his thumb and index finger.

'It's not about what I think. It's the law.' The first sign of impatience escapes Timothy and his words come out harsher than he intended.

Innocent crosses his arms over his chest. 'Are you gay?' he asks. He peers at the inspector, looking him up and down suspiciously. The other boys start to snigger.

'What?' Timothy's forehead wrinkles.

'I'm asking if you're gay, man?' Innocent grins, enjoying the confusion he's created. He's like a different person when his teeth are on display, handsome and boyish.

'Of course not! And even if I was, what's it to you?'

Innocent moves his mouth in doubtful circles. 'I don't know, man. You look gay.' He turns to his friends. 'What do you think?'

'He's a batty-man,' comes the verdict.

Timothy looks around. He feels the sweat break out on the back of his neck. He doesn't have anything against gay people, but it's embarrassing to be called something you're not in public like this. And by a bunch of teenagers at that.

'I'm not gay, OK? Are you going to pay the fare or what?'

'Prove it.' Innocent's face has set back into its usual scornful expression.

'What?'

'I don't believe you're not gay, so prove it.' His tongue rolls with pleasure in his mouth. He's enjoying the shift in the balance of power, relishing the amusement and approval of his peers. He's aware that every single person in the carriage is listening to the conversation: no one's phone is ringing, nobody is talking. There is silence, and under that a very real interest in how this exchange is going to pan out. Innocent feels it like a force, the way actors on stage must feel the power of an audience.

'You can't prove you're not gay and I can't prove I'm a student, so which of us is wrong?' Innocent raises himself up to his full height. He's taller than his peers and the inspector. He's so used to slouching, mainly so his jeans will stay on, that it's always a pleasant surprise to discover he can look down on the adults who try to cow him. He extends a hand, offering the two-pound coin again.

Timothy is speechless. He stands with his jaw clenched and considers the absolute lack of logic in the boy's argument. Part of him knows he should take the lower fare and go. You can't win with these sorts of people. Another part of him can't accept that this behaviour should be allowed. The inspector's face hardens and he sticks out his chest. 'Pay the three pounds now or you're getting a fine,' he says.

'Look at this clown! How much you getting paid to do this? Move on. Go hassle someone else.' Innocent turns away and presents his back to the inspector.

Timothy stares at it. He starts tapping on his machine again. 'I need your name and address.' He's fully prepared to be given the wrong details, but he feels he has to go through the motions.

Innocent speaks without turning. 'I don't have to tell you shit. I'm ready to buy a ticket and you don't want to sell me one.' He raises a hand, the coin gleams in his fingers. It's a new one. The inner steel circle is bright silver, the ring around it shiny yellow. 'Take it or leave it,' he says.

Timothy's options are narrowing. He looks towards the window, trying to judge how far they might be from the next stop, but he can't see clearly past all the people. He guesses it'll be a minute, maybe a minute and half, before they reach the next station. The kid will probably bolt off the train there. That or the whole gang might push *him* out: that's happened to Timothy once before.

'Oi, batty-man!' Comfort looks over his shoulder at the inspector. 'Why you still hanging around here? Get on with your job. Maybe you can find a white man to pick on for a change.'

'Right. This is your last chance.' Timothy chews on his lower lip. He really doesn't want to do what he'll have to do next.

Innocent and all the other guys ignore him now, turning up the volume on their mobiles again.

When Timothy starts walking away, squeezing along the crowded aisle, it looks like Innocent has won. Then they see Timothy put a key into the glass box protecting the alarm. A flap opens on one side and he reaches in to pull the lever.

Chapter Seven

That morning Innocent Babatunde had got up as usual at 07:15. The moment the alarm went, he was out of bed. Not for him the snooze setting going off every eight to ten minutes. His sisters used that, his mother too. They set the alarm at least half an hour early so they could spend the extra time lounging, pretending to themselves that they were getting a lie-in. Seemed stupid to Innocent. Lying around half awake and knowing you had to be up soon. Plain dumb, actually. Better to sleep as long as you could and rise when you had to.

He was the only one in the house who didn't share a room. His mother, Ivie, slept with the baby, Ruth, and his two sisters, Adanna and Charity, shared a room. Innocent's space was small, just about holding a single bed and a desk. His clothes were stored in drawers under the bed. His trainers, all six pairs, were lined up along the wall near the door.

The bed was always made; not very neatly, but made. That was one thing his mother had insisted on since he was a little boy, so he'd got into the habit. It was a reflex, now, when he got out of bed, to drag the duvet with him. Then he'd grab two corners, fling the whole fluffy mass into the air and let it settle back down on the bed. He liked to think that that was about as domestic as he got, but his mum would argue that he's also a very good babysitter.

Above the bed a Nigerian flag hung down from the ceiling. Innocent had never been there, nor had his mother, but his grandparents had come from that country, and his dad had been born there too. That was all he knew about his dad, who'd left his mother when she was pregnant. According to his mother, Innocent's father had gone back to Lagos because he got tired of being a black man in London. He was always a black man in that city, never just a man. He wanted to go somewhere where his colour didn't matter. Ivie didn't feel the same and hadn't followed him. The man had left and made no effort to stay in touch or honour his duties as a father. Over the years, the saying 'makes me want to run off to Lagos' had become a standard expression for anything bad or annoying in the family.

The duvet had floated almost perfectly back onto the bed when Innocent's mum came into the room carrying Ruth.

'What happened to knocking before you enter?' Innocent tucked his hands under his armpits. He was wearing boxers and a baggy, torn vest. Sleep was still crusted in the corners of his eyes.

'You got nothing I haven't seen before.' Ivie set Ruth on the bed and gestured to Innocent that he should take hold of her feeding bottle. 'I've got to go.' She was starting an hour earlier at the nursing home where she worked. 'Charity will take over when she's out of the shower.'

'She better be out in two minutes or I'm gonna be late.' He got down on his knees and leaned over Ruth, making gargling sounds. She smiled and milk leaked from the little pink corner of her mouth. Innocent used the edge of her bib to wipe away the dribble. His mum watched for a second, her heart trapped by the strange loveliness of her boy-man playing with her baby. Ruth was a happy little accident, born seventeen years after Innocent. Ivie was engaged to marry the girl's father and they hoped to have enough money for a small wedding by the summer.

Innocent leaned forward on his elbows and nuzzled his nose against Ruth's forehead. He crooned to her as if he was rapping:

'Who's so tiny?

Who's so sweet?

Who's got the yummiest little feet?'

He pretended to gobble her up.

'Hmmm, what a treat!'

Ruth stopped sucking on the teat and smiled again. Her chubby arms and legs wriggled happily, the creamy palms and soles fluttering like silk handkerchiefs being waved in welcome.

Ivie couldn't leave without giving them both a kiss. As her lips touched Innocent's head he said, 'Can I have five pounds, Mum?'

'What you need more money for?' Her hands went to her hips, which were a bit too wide for her body. Other than that, she was a slender woman with a long neck and a weakness for hair straightening. At the moment she was sporting a short bob with a fringe, but her hair had been exposed to so many chemicals it was as dry and stiff as wire. 'You already got your cash for the week.'

'I just need a bit extra.' Innocent went on playing with Ruth. He needed to scrape together enough dosh to buy a new railcard somehow. By wangling from his mother and sisters he hoped to be able to afford one today or tomorrow.

Ivie leaned over, trying to look him in the eye. 'I hope you're not in any kind of trouble, boy?'

'Why do you always go assuming the worst? The way you get, Mum . . . makes me want to go running to Lagos.' His tone was just the right side of hurt to get his mother's sympathy. Besides, Ivie was in too much of a hurry to spend time probing further.

'I'll leave something on the kitchen table.' Ivie blew a kiss to Ruth and backed out of the room. 'Make sure you're back by eight tonight. I'm doing a double-shift and Charity's working nights this week, so you'll need to mind Ruth.'

'What about Adanna?' He turned from the bed but his mother was already out of the door.

'She's got a date,' Ivie called.

'I'm just the plug in this family! It's always me stopping the gap while all you ladies do what you want!' There was no response to his outcry. He faced Ruth again. Her bottle was almost empty. He caught sight of the time on his clock and yelled to his older sister to get out of the bathroom. Then he pressed his mouth to Ruth's stomach and blew against it, making the farting sounds she loved.

A minute later Charity appeared in a blue dressing gown with a yellow towel wrapped around her head. He jumped up and pushed past her. 'I'm gonna miss my train because of you.'

'Like that really bothers you. What about the times you're so late you miss the whole day?'

She picked up Ruth and followed him out of the room and down the corridor.

'Shu'up. What do you know?' He stopped by the bathroom door. 'By the way, can I borrow a tenner?'

'No! You already owe me twenty pounds.' She had Ruth over one shoulder, rubbing the baby's back as she tried to burp her.

'I'll pay it back, I swear. I need it badly.'

'Get a job like the rest of us if you're so desperate.' She disappeared into the living room so only her voice drifted down the tunnel of the corridor towards Innocent.

'It's not like I haven't tried!' He was about to shut the bathroom door when Charity appeared again. She looked slender even under the thick towelling wrap of her gown. 'No one wants to hire a black guy,' Innocent went on, hoping she was changing her mind. 'They see me and they think, there's trouble. They've all got a problem with—'

'Oh, enough now!' Charity bent down to pick up Ruth's muslin cloth, which she'd accidentally dropped earlier. 'The only place there's a problem is in your head!' At Charity's shoulder Ruth let out a long burp. It sounded like the sort of noise only an old, fat man could produce.

'You're going to be sorry you ever said that.' Innocent slammed the bathroom door shut and from behind it shouted once more, 'You'll be sorry!'

Chapter Eight

The train comes to a stop with a jolt and Helen loses her balance, flopping forwards onto the man seated in front of her. It's only Kerm's quick reaction, reaching out to grab her shoulders, that prevents her from collapsing onto him fully.

'Sorry!' She tries to stand again, but it feels like everybody else in the carriage is pushing up behind her. She remains suspended over Kerm, one hand clutching his arm for support, the other holding onto her phone. Her handbag slides off her shoulder, the strap lodging in the crook of her elbow while the bulk of the bag falls on Kerm's thigh.

'Would you like to sit down?' He shifts as if to get up from his seat.

Helen doesn't hear the words but understands the action. 'No! No, I'm fine. Thanks.' She manages to straighten up, shakes her hair out of her face and thrusts her phone into the pocket of her coat.

'Are you sure?' Kerm's bottom hovers just

above the seat. Thick eyebrows rise over his dark brown eyes.

Helen pulls her earphones out as he repeats the question. 'I'm OK, really.' She's not sure why she's insisting when it would be nicer to sit down. One of her ankles is turned at an odd angle, making it hard to balance. She almost falls again as the train lurches into motion once more.

The man gives her a smile as he settles into the seat again. His grin is boyish: a row of perfect teeth set off charmingly by the chipped tip of one central upper incisor. She studies him as he goes back to reading his newspaper. The corners of his eyes and mouth are untouched by lines. Although his face lacks the seriousness of wrinkles, there is an authority in the hard set of his jaw and a confidence in the tousled mess of his overgrown hair. She can tell he's tall from the way his head looms higher than all of the other seated passengers. His legs stick out into the aisle on either side of her, like barriers.

Without the protection of her earphones, Helen registers the din around her for the first time. In the conversations she overhears, every word seems to be followed by an exclamation mark: 'Sandra! That's! The! Wrong! One!' She feels weary just listening. Suddenly she can't wait to be off the train and at her destination. She notices that the train's slowed down again. She thinks they must be approaching a station, but suddenly they draw to a sharp halt right in the middle of nowhere.

Outside there is only a bland darkness. It is the typical dark of cities: soft at the edges, its purity corrupted by the electric grid, which stretches through every park and down every dead-end street.

Helen looks left and right, as if for an explanation for the stoppage, but there's no announcement – nothing – and nobody else seems bothered. The school kids banter away as if they have all the time in the world, and the few other passengers Helen can see appear absorbed in their newspapers or mobiles. Meanwhile, she feels like her shoes have been replaced by stilts and that she might topple over any second if someone doesn't budge and give her a bit more room.

She should have taken the seat when the man offered it to her. She glances at him again and realises that her handbag is still lodged on his thigh. She pulls at the strap and hoists it onto her shoulder, using the chance to try to wangle herself a bit more space. It doesn't work. Helen sighs and wonders if she could do a good enough job of pretending to faint so he'll give her his seat. Acting has never been her strength. She'd probably start laughing and give herself away. It might be better to tap on his knee and tell him she's changed her mind, except he'd probably think she's a weirdo.

She could brush against him, as if by accident, and then? Helen tells herself to stop being silly. She reaches into her pocket for her phone, but the focus of her mind remains fixed on the seated man. His hands are poised just a few centimetres away from her. She likes the grip of his fingers on the newspaper: strong fingers with neat nails. They look like an artist's hands. She can picture them holding a brush, splashing paint on large canvases. Part of one sturdy wrist is exposed under the black sleeves of his shirt and jacket. Helen imagines holding hands with him. He seems trustworthy somehow.

Her mum, Sheila, would laugh now if she could read Helen's thoughts. It's just like her youngest child to judge someone's honesty on the shape of his hands. No doubt Helen has good intuition (didn't she always doubt Danny?), but you can't rely on gut feelings alone when it comes to men. After all, there are other more telling signs. A woman must learn to look out for those and say goodbye to her instincts.

Sure, following instincts might give you a nice feeling, but instincts don't guarantee you the 'big three', as Sheila calls them: a three-storey house, a new car every three years and three holidays a year.

Helen takes a deep breath and tells herself to get a grip. She's surprised she has any power at all for positive thinking about men after what she found out this afternoon. She grasps at the handrail with her right hand to steady herself and activates her phone with the left. There's a fresh list of postings on her Facebook page:

Charles Parker needs a second body so he can run a 2-shifts' lifestyle. Let one sleep at night and the other in the day.

Tobias Felwood has worked out a direct link between his Ladyship's stress levels and the amount of clothes left lying around the flat . . .

Helen's eyes dart towards the man sitting opposite her again. She notices that he hasn't turned a single page of his newspaper. When he blinks, his eyes shut slowly and deliberately, as if there's some grit in them. She pictures herself blowing gently into his eyes, the way her mum used to when she was little. For a second she thinks he's winking at her because he closes just one eye, but then he does the same with the other, switching back and forth a couple of times, as if he's testing his vision.

Then he looks up and catches her staring. She averts her gaze quickly, surprised at the rapid beating of her heart. With her left thumb she starts to type in another Facebook update:

Helen is having crazy thoughts and wondering whether to act on them . . .

All of a sudden, the door between their carriage and the one behind swings open. Three schoolboys with shaved heads and pierced ears start pushing through the crowd. It would be hard to say exactly how old they are. Their bodies have the cultivated swagger of late teenagers trying to pull off a macho manliness. One of them still has cheeks that hint at puppy fat, but they all have eyes that have seen more than they should, and mouths that seem tight with an anger that seems centuries old.

'Make way. Make way. Niggaz comin' thru!' Jostling and shoving the boys edge forward in single file. Other passengers struggle to give them space, but it isn't easy.

'Move!' The lips of the tallest one curl over the

word in a snarl. All three keep glancing behind them as though expecting someone to be in hot pursuit.

'Make way for a nigga,' the third boy in line shouts. He holds his plastic school bag aloft, like a flag. The three diagonal lines of branding on it might be some kind of secret code to signal that the crowd should part for these guys like the waters of the Red Sea did for Moses in the Bible. Indeed, people oblige, adults and school kids alike. The train passengers fall silent, lean back and huddle closer together, to let the little tornado through.

The boys are near Helen now, in the most packed part of the carriage, and their progress isn't as quick as they'd like.

'Come on! Move!' The tall one at the front elbows a schoolgirl and steps on Helen's foot as he tries to get past.

'We can't move!' Helen says. 'There's nowhere to go.' Her words are automatic, more a thought that's spoken by mistake than an attempt to be defiant. But the boys don't know that. To them, she's the first person who's spoken, offered any kind of resistance. And what's more, she doesn't look like the type you'd expect to squeak, let alone present any kind of challenge.

'Shu'up, you fat bitch.' The tall boy's fist

swings out, accidentally catching Helen's face above the right cheekbone, near her eye.

Helen stumbles and falls onto Kerm again. There's darkness, then coloured blobs appear in front of her. She hears someone utter an indignant, 'Hey!' which is followed by sniggers, then she feels herself shoved again as another male voice says, 'Yeah, lose some weight, bitch.'

Kerm barely has time to grasp what's going on. He's thinking that somebody has to stop these idiots. He himself can't see a thing or move a limb. He's buried in a flowery, vanilla-spiced scent as the woman tumbles onto him. The wool of her sweater tickles his nose, her elbow digs into the side of his neck, her bag hits his head and her phone slips, like a smooth brick, into his crotch. His newspaper and left hand are crushed against his chest. The woman is quite heavy. The sudden impact of her body against his leaves Kerm winded, but still alert enough to call out in dismay at her attackers.

Nobody else resists as the boys pass roughly by. The show of violence has made the boys appear all the more frightening. The tall one sucks in his cheeks and curls his upper lip. If anyone had dared to look into his face they would have seen defiance shining in his eyes: And? What you gonna do about it?

All the adults are suddenly very busy staring out of the train windows or checking their watches. They pull in their stomachs and hold their breath, trying to take up as little room as possible until the boys have passed. Some of the school children seem a little shocked and taken aback, but most watch what's happened with neutral expressions. A few even laugh. At the top of the carriage the boys find that the door to the next section of the train is jammed. The tall one pushes against it. He swears and tries again, but it doesn't budge. His friends have a go, but they have no luck either. They look at each other and they're all thinking the same thing: Fuck!

Chapter Nine

Kerm helps Helen get off him, holding her forearms and gently pushing her upright. If the incident hadn't been so horrible he might have jokingly asked if he had 'runway' written on his forehead, because it's the second time she's landed on him. But he saw how the blow was dealt and he knows that as the shock wears off, pain will take its place.

With adrenalin pumping through his own body, Kerm manages, somehow, to slide out of his seat and settle the woman into his place.

'I'm sorry.' He keeps apologising as though it's his fault. He should have made her take his seat before. He should have just got up and forced her to sit down. 'I'm really sorry.'

Helen shakes her head at the man fussing over her, as if the simple turn of her head can erase his regret. Her lips tremble. She's dizzy. It feels like someone's lit a fire under her right cheek-bone. She blinks rapidly, trying to stop herself from crying. She feels like sobbing, falling into someone's arms and wailing, Why do these things always happen to me?

Helen was the one who was jumped on by a man on a motorbike one night during her school French exchange trip to Marseilles. She's the one whom two freckle-faced youths followed across Wandsworth Common in broad daylight, repeatedly kicking their football at her legs. If those incidents weren't enough, she's also the one who, just last year, had a loaf of French bread snatched from her hand near a market in Paris, only to find herself whipped on the bottom moments later by the very same baguette. She was hit so hard the stick of bread broke in half. On top of all that, let's not forget, she's the one who's been plagued for months by upsetting late-night phone calls from her disgusting brother-in-law.

Helen's made it her mission not to let anybody she knows take advantage of her, but it seems as though total strangers do so pretty regularly. She remains hunched over in the seat. Her elbows are wedged into her waist, her fingers pressed against her temples.

'Excuse me?' Kerm crouches down to get the woman's attention.

Helen lifts her head. Her cheeks are wet and her nose is running.

Kerm reaches into his pocket for a tissue, knowing he probably doesn't have one. For a doctor, he's remarkably unprepared for emergencies. Even at home he keeps little medicine, apart from a bottle of aspirin.

The woman seated to Helen's left squeezes her arm, hands her a tissue and murmurs something about hooligans. The awkward silence that filled the carriage as the boys powered through has been replaced by a low but lively hum. There's still a faint air of embarrassment amongst those near to Helen, but on the whole people are getting back to normal. They shuffle their newspapers and tut impatiently at the train's lack of progress and the driver's lack of explanation.

'How's that eye doing?' asks Kerm, leaning in to take a closer look. Helen's right eyelid has already puffed up a bit. In ten to fifteen minutes bruising will start to show. Already, he can tell, she's taking care not to blink. Her hazel eyes, streaked with gold and green, are fixed on him.

Kerm goes into doctor-mode and extends a hand. His index finger presses gently along the top of her eyebrow and moves down to her cheekbone. If there were paint on his fingertip the action would have left a line of coloured dots along the right side of Helen's face.

The way he examines her is reassuring. There's

a practical confidence in his touch, like he knows what he's doing. So Helen doesn't flinch or tell him to stop, even though she's aware that it's odd to have a stranger do this in the middle of a crowded train carriage.

'Can you see OK out of that eye?' he asks. Kerm continues with the questions even after she nods. 'No double vision? No floaters?'

Helen shakes her head. The pain is now spreading across her face.

'It might be an idea to have an X-ray. Make sure your zygoma – your cheekbone –' he adds, aware that he's lapsed into doctor's speak, 'isn't damaged'. Kerm suddenly realises how odd he must seem, offering his opinions like this without being asked. 'Sorry, I should have explained, I'm a doctor . . . in case you're wondering. Dr Kerm Vora.'

Helen nods as if she's already guessed. The throbbing at her right eye is getting worse. It's as if someone's playing drums on her eyeball.

'I'm sorry I can't give you something for the pain. I don't have anything on me.' He flaps the empty pockets of his coat, whose hem, he notices, is brushing along the dirty floor of the carriage. Kerm stands upright for a moment, then bends down again. He sets a hand on one of the armrests on either side of Helen to support himself. It's not a very dignified position: knees bent and bum stuck out as though he's getting ready to take a dump.

There are some irritated glances from nearby passengers who have to budge a little because of him. All Helen can see are his clean-shaven face and broad shoulders, which seem even wider in the thick wool coat he's wearing. She notices the way his hair, which is tucked behind his ears, flicks out under his long earlobes.

'Thanks for your help.' As she speaks Helen becomes aware of a metallic taste in her mouth. Her impulse is to spit, but that's hardly possible right now.

Kerm sees the slight shift in her features and catches sight of a red wash on her teeth as her lips part slightly before pressing together again. 'You may have a wound on the inside of your cheek. Your teeth probably cut into the inside of your mouth when his hand hit your face.'

'Here, have this.' A girl with a high ponytail and too much eye make-up holds out a half-full bottle of mineral water.

'Thanks.' Kerm takes the drink, which is still cold, and passes it to Helen.

Her fingers close over the ribbed plastic bottle, but she doesn't raise it to her mouth. The idea of washing down the warm iron-y taste with water makes her feel sick. Why the idea of swallowing your own blood is so unpleasant, she has no idea. Your body if full of the stuff anyway, she tells herself, but the thought still makes her shiver.

Kerm brings his face level with Helen's. 'Try holding the bottle to your cheek; the cold might help. It's not going to look pretty tomorrow.' She can feel his breath on her mouth as he talks. Her jaw trembles with emotion at his concern, at the kindness in his dark eyes.

'But don't fret about it!' He sees anxiety pulse across her features. 'It's not going to change the fact that you have a very nice face. You'll be fine in a week or two.' He looks in the direction the boys went. He has no idea that they are just three or four metres away, behind thirty-or-so standing passengers, still trying to un-jam the door to the next carriage. 'They shouldn't be allowed to get away with this. We could raise the alarm with the driver. Maybe try and get them caught?' Nearby, he can see a red lever behind its protective glass box.

Helen is already shaking her head.

'I'd be happy to give a witness statement. I'm sure other people would too.' He glances around, but if anyone has overheard they're not jumping up to volunteer. 'We could raise the alarm. Someone will get on board at the next station to see what's up. It's not right that those boys should go scot-free.'

'No.' The police may well think there's something wrong with *her* at this rate. Helen's mum, Sheila, will definitely think she's to blame. It will be too much hassle, she decides, and she can't cope with that as well, at the moment. It occurs to Helen that she's probably going to have a black eye for Jill's party. 'No,' she repeats. Her words sound like they're being gargled out because of the mouthful of blood she can't bring herself to swallow.

'However you like.' Kerm stands tall again. 'You should just sit tight for a few minutes. Take some deep breaths.'

He realises he's still holding the woman's phone. He'd kept it clutched between his thighs while he'd helped her sit down, then he'd slipped it into his pocket. He takes it out now, ready to give it back, but she's looking into her lap again. Her shoulders heave slowly as she follows his breathing instructions and she has a wad of tissues pressed over her lips.

He sees how her hair falls in an extreme side parting. How glossy her hair is. Brightness dazzles through the thick strands like flashes of lightning. It's as if he's never seen a woman's head before. The straight line of scalp that's visible somehow has more erotic appeal than the longest legs or the most perfect breasts. He wants to run his tongue along that line, and down over her forehead to the sharp ski-jump bridge of her nose until her lips . . .

Kerm has to catch himself again. He tenses all his muscles, as if that will stop his thoughts from wandering. What is wrong with him today? Is this what death at close quarters does? Forces you to obsess about sex? It makes a twisted kind of sense: promoting the cycle of life is our best weapon against death.

Kerm feels ashamed, guilty, sad and a touch horny at the same time. If his grandfather's death has shown him anything, it's that emotions can co-exist in the most bizarre combinations.

Chapter Ten

In ungracious moments, Kerm would wonder whether his family would have been as pleased to see him at the hospital if he wasn't a doctor. These thoughts usually occurred when he was standing on the windy, dimly lit platform, waiting for the last train back into central London.

His medical expertise was what the relatives seemed to relish. Within seconds of his arrival at each visit to his grandfather's hospital bed, consultants' comments, newly prescribed drugs and the tiniest changes in Baoji's appearance or diet would be listed for Kerm's benefit, followed by, 'But he's going to be fine, isn't he?'

It quickly became clear that Kerm's professional opinion was required only to confirm signs of improvement. There was no room for pessimism around Baoji's bed. The bunches of flowers, piles of fruit and lines of cards seemed to have been arranged to wall out negativity. Even the old man himself was not allowed a say in how he was faring.

Several days before his death he had begun

to predict it. 'I'm going . . .' he had whispered to his son Rajan one night in Kerm's presence. 'I'll be gone soon.'

'Don't be silly.' Rajan stood up and began plumping the pillows at his father's head. The shape of Baoji's skull, every curve and hollow, was visible under the loose folds of skin.

'I'm going,' Baoji repeated.

'Yes, going to get better.' Rajan shot Kerm a look, as if he ought to know how to put an end to this sort of nonsense.

Kerm glanced at the floor. He noticed all the scratches on the lino from the wheels of the trolleys bringing meals, and the beds being rolled to and from the operating theatre.

'No, I'll be gone.' Baoji spoke with his eyes shut. His eyeballs twitched under thin lids.

'Stop talking like that.' Rajan gripped the metal rail of the bed frame. His eyes were red and puffy from lack of sleep. All the lines in his face were deepened by worry. 'Everything will be fine. You tell him, Kerm.'

'I'll get the nurse.' Kerm stood up. 'Maybe they can up his morphine or something.' As if that was the answer.

Kerm walked off, aware of his father's discomfort. How do you tell your father that his dad is about to die? Maybe if they'd had a different relationship it would have been easier. On one level Kerm understood the family's unwillingness to face the truth. But at the same time, by denying the old man's prophecy, his family was missing out on the chance to face the end with him, to say goodbye properly, to let him go more easily. It wasn't even as if the family had resolved their differences and were all on good terms with one another. There was still lots of unfinished business between them.

Nothing, for instance, had been said regarding Sam's sudden return from the other side of the world. It was as though the simple fact that he was there was enough. Maybe it was, Kerm told himself as he walked down the corridor, past the waste disposal room with warning signs on the door. Maybe the Vora family had it right. Perhaps his own preference for analysis and discussion was strange. Hadn't his father once called him a sissy? Saying he'd spent too much time in female company and had turned out just like his mother? Who was he to judge?

In the last days of Baoji's life, normal rules about visiting hours had been waived for the Vora family: a sure sign that the end was near. Late on a Monday night, Kerm had sat on one side of the hospital bed. Directly opposite, his father and aunt kept their nightly vigil over Baoji's wasting body under the bleached white sheets.

Kerm had listened whilst the two of them talked about their father. They remarked on how he wouldn't let anyone leave the house without sharing a shot of something with them first. It didn't matter who the visitor was, the Granthi from the local gurdwara or the widow from down the road, and it didn't matter what time of day they came. Every guest had some kind of alcoholic drink thrust into their hands.

It was interesting to see how, already, the past was being re-cast. There was no mention of Baoji's problems with the tipple, or his tendency to overdo it.

'He never drank alone,' whispered Veena, squeezing the old man's hand. One of the nurses had mentioned that, towards the end, it was better to keep a gentle hold on the patient. Then they didn't have the sense that they couldn't let go. The nurse had said it made it easier for the dying to leave if they felt they had your consent. Ever since then Veena had been keeping an extra-tight grip on her father.

'No, he liked company,' Rajan agreed. 'He enjoyed making toasts. He loved quoting Oscar

Wilde, do you remember? "Work is the curse of the drinking class."'

'It was all from that book you gave him!' Veena jabbed playfully at her brother's arm. Rajan had once bought their father a small volume called *Cheers!,* which was full of famous quotations about alcohol. Baoji had memorised many of them and would recite them regularly as he lifted another glass of whisky to his lips. 'There was another Wilde quote he liked a lot . . .' Veena pulled a pin out of her bun and stuck it back in more securely. 'What was it?' She clicked her front teeth together, trying to remember.

'"Moderation is a fatal thing – nothing succeeds like excess,"' Rajan said. The sharp point of his turban looked slightly off centre. It was hard to tell if that was because it hadn't been tied perfectly, or if it was because of the angle at which his head was tenderly tilted as he watched his father.

'Yes!' Veena smiled. 'And the Churchill one.' It was coming back to her now. '"I have taken more out of alcohol than alcohol has taken out of me." Baoji loved that.'

'You have to show me this book some time,' Kerm said to his dad.

They talked in hushed tones so as not to disturb the three other patients in the small ward. Every bed was partitioned by a curtain hanging from a mobile rail, and from behind each flimsy cloth, the hum of life support machines and the painful sighs of laboured breath could be heard: a soundtrack of ebbing life.

'That was the beauty of Baoji's drinking.' Veena stood up and smoothed the sheets. 'The sharing.'

'Yeah,' Kerm said, not sure whether the observation was intended to be ironic or nostalgic. 'He even offered me a drink when I got here earlier.'

Kerm had arrived before his father. He had been keeping Veena company for a few minutes when Baoji had stirred into one of his rare moments of wakefulness. Veena had pushed her nephew's head close to his grandfather's, exhorting the old man to acknowledge the younger one. Baoji had appeared to recognise him, or at least Kerm's name triggered something. Who could tell how much the dying man could see from behind the milky film of his cataracts? In a faint, rasping voice, like tissue paper being crushed, Baoji had welcomed Kerm. Then, as if he were still presiding over the minibar in his living room, he'd asked his grandson what he'd like to drink.

'You know,' Kerm's musings continued, 'the

first time he gave me alcohol I was well below the legal age.' He'd been twelve when Baoji had poured him a whisky on the rocks. Not that Kerm had drunk it, but he still remembered the casual ceremony with which his grandfather had handed him the crystal glass. Inside it the amber liquid had glowed, while the ice cubes had snapped and crackled as if they too were excited by the gesture.

'He's one of a kind.' Veena pressed a palm against the old man's forehead.

They all lapsed into silence for a while, until someone started calling out from one of the neighbouring beds: 'Ted. Ted?' The voice was feeble, but it sounded urgent.

Rajan and Veena looked at Kerm as though he should know what to do. His reaction was to turn to the nurses' desk a few metres down the corridor, only to find it temporarily deserted.

As the calls continued Kerm shrugged. 'There's no medicine to stop you wanting someone.'

The voice went on every few seconds for another minute, 'Ted? Ted?' Then it stopped. Almost immediately the bed next door to Baoji's creaked and a voice abruptly enquired, 'Dead? Who's dead?'

Kerm had to slam his hand over his mouth to stifle the sound of his laughter. He sat shaking for several minutes, his eyes streaming, his body convulsing uncontrollably with giggles. It was infectious and Rajan and Veena joined in. To anyone watching from a distance it might have seemed like the figures huddled around bed number two were rocking with grief.

When a nurse came by a short while later they had barely composed themselves; one just had to catch another's eye and they would be off again. 'He was calling for help.' Kerm's words sounded choked as he pointed in the direction from which the calls for Ted had come. The nurse disappeared behind the curtain, and when she emerged again Kerm knew what had happened. He could read it in her posture: the slight rounding of her shoulders, the sudden briskness in her stride.

The hard fact filled the room like a blast of cold air. Kerm had shivered and his dad had stiffened. Veena had reached over and wrapped both her hands around Baoji's. She squeezed tight, holding on for dear life.

Chapter Eleven

Innocent, Blessing and Comfort give up on the swing door that is supposed to be their escape route to the next compartment of the train and instead make their way to one of the main exits. People move out of the way without being told now. The boys simply choose a direction and lift a foot and a pathway is clear in seconds.

At the sliding double doors, they try to squeeze their fingers between the join and push them apart. People watch furtively, peeking out from behind their newspapers. Everyone's wondering what they're up to. Are they just impatient? Do they intend to jump off the train and run across the tracks? A little area has cleared around the boys.

'This is shit.' Innocent stares out of the glass that covers half the door. Not much is visible outside. A train hurtles by in the opposite direction, a long ribbon of light being pulled through the night.

Innocent's stomach growls. He hadn't had breakfast that morning because of the rush he'd been in. For lunch he'd had the special meal at Chicken n' Ribs – four drumsticks and chips for a pound – but that felt like ages ago.

The rustle of the intercom fills the carriage. Everyone stops talking and turns an ear towards the ceiling, where the speakers are located. The driver's voice informs them, 'Ladies and gentlemen, sorry about the delay. The emergency alarm has been activated on this train. We're just waiting for some support to arrive at the next station before we pull up there. It shouldn't be much longer now. Thanks for your patience.'

A wave of groans rides the length of the carriage. Innocent pulls his jeans up a fraction, Blessing flips his hoodie over his head and Comfort rolls his shoulders forwards and dips his chin towards his chest. They all know what this means.

Innocent's face twitches as he thinks of the inspector. 'That clown has messed up everything.' He kicks at the metal frame of the door, then checks the tip of his brand-new white trainers to make sure none of the grime has come off on them.

'Here, let me try.' Comfort signals that the other two should mask him. He pulls something out from the inner pocket of his puffer jacket, steps up to the doors and jams an object between them. It's a knife. One flick of the handle and eight centimetres of steel blade snaps into view.

If they can get off the train here, Comfort reckons, they'll be fine. He knows this strip of track well from earlier graffiti-spraying sessions. He has run from side to side dodging the police and passing trains before. They could do it again, if they could just get the hell out.

Kerm can't help glancing at Helen's phone, which is still in his possession. It keeps lighting up, its screen bursting with a blue the colour of summer skies. Each time a new statement appears on the screen. It's Facebook, he realises. Her Facebook page. He scans it, looking for her name. Helen Summers: he sees it in the top left-hand corner. Helen. His eyes swing guiltily away from the screen. He clears his throat, hoping she might look his way, but Helen is too busy trying to spit discreetly into the crumple of tissues pressed between her mouth and palm. She manages somehow. Then, afraid to look at what might have come out, she crushes the paper into her fist whilst wiping her mouth with the other hand.

The slim cable of her earphones is splayed around her neck like a futuristic garland. Kerm notices that its connecting end has been pulled from the phone and is dangling between her legs. He bends down to pick it up, his hand brushing her knee in the process. She lifts her head and sees the man reconnect her headphones to the phone.

'I seem to have ended up with this in the scramble.' He waves the gadget at her but doesn't hand it over right away. They're both aware of the thread-like piece of plastic hanging between them: a delicate connection. Helen makes no move to take ownership of the phone either.

'Thanks again.' At least she can talk properly now.

Kerm bends down towards her. 'How are you doing?' There's a little smudge of blood at the corner of her mouth.

'Not the best.' She's sure she must look terrible. The right side of her face feels huge.

'Are you sure you can see all right? How many fingers?' He holds her phone up.

She laughs, then quickly stops as pain shoots through her cheek and eye.

'You'd best watch that smile.' His lips press together in mock seriousness. 'Normally it's lethal for other people, but for the next few days you'll be its victim too, so take care.'

'When people ask me why I look so glum I'll

tell them it's because of doctor's orders: I'm under strict instructions not to smile.'

'Good.' Kerm nods. 'I like obedient patients.'

'How do you know if they really listen to you? It's not as if you can check up on them.' Helen runs a finger along her lips, which feel dry and cracked. God, she must look awful. She has no idea why this man is being so nice to her.

'Oh, you can tell. You get better at it over the years. You can detect when there's a self-destructive streak in people.' He straightens up again. His back is hurting from all the bending and he's starting to feel too hot. He shrugs off his coat, followed by his suit jacket.

'So you don't think I'm one of those?' Helen's eyebrows rise, only to fall the next instant. Her forehead creases and her free hand goes protectively to the aching spot.

Kerm winces in sympathy. 'This injury is going to give you good practice at keeping a poker face. As for what kind of patient you are . . .' He scratches the dip between his nose and upper lip. 'It's actually too soon to say. It might be an idea for me to check up on you. I could do that if you give me the number of this thing.' He thrusts her phone towards her. His eyes do that funny wink-thing again: first one eye shutting and opening, and then the other.

Helen takes the phone from him and their fingers touch. A flush of heat spreads through her body, as if someone has opened an oven door deep inside her. She doesn't know how to respond. She's never given her number to a complete stranger. It feels . . . like gambling. Like putting all your chips on the roulette table in one go and then watching the wheel spin.

'Think about it.' Kerm stretches to his full height. His forward manner has left him surprised and he can tell she's taken aback too.

She fiddles with the phone.

'Are you left-handed?' Kerm asks.

'Sort of.' Helen can't explain that the right one, which she normally uses, is occupied with hiding a lump of soiled tissues. 'You can put in your name and number if you like.' She passes the phone back to him.

'I haven't used one of these touchy-things before.' He presses hesitantly on the letters visible through the screen. 'It's easy!' He smiles as his name is typed out and then saved. He does the same with his number. 'Nifty.' He tries to get back to the main menu, but ends up in her text messages instead. 'I'd better give it back to you before I delete something.'

She takes it without looking. On the screen is the message she's written to Jill. It's asking whether to 'send' or 'save' again. As Helen's fingers close around the phone, her thumb presses down on 'send'.

Innocent hits his fists together impatiently. He catches sight of an older woman nearby peeking at him and his friends. 'Hey, what's got your eye?' He jerks his chin at her.

She turns away quickly, clutching her bag closer. Her pearls are the same colour as her hair, and now both match the wan look on her face.

'Hey, lady.' Innocent steps up to her. 'Why you holding that bag so tight? You think I'm gonna steal it coz I'm black?'

She shakes her head, the loose skin at her neck flapping slightly. Her knuckles stand out around the strap of her blue leather handbag.

'Check these people!' Innocent waves over his friends. He doesn't see how Comfort gives the doors one last shove only to have the blade of his knife snap and slip outside. He's left holding the handle, which has two inches of metal hanging off it. Comfort curses under his breath and folds the damaged weapon into his hand. It's so reduced in size that the broken tip of blade is hardly visible in his clenched palm, which he draws under the over-long sleeves of his jacket.

'Just check them all!' Innocent throws back

his head and laughs. 'See how shook they all are.' His voice fills the compartment and then fades into the unnatural silence that follows. 'Yeah, yeah, hide away your phones, people, the black boy might nick them.'

Kerm recognises the voice. He stops talking to Helen and peers towards the far end of the carriage. Over the wave of heads he sees the boys. 'It's the same guys who got you,' he says quietly.

Innocent takes a good long look at everyone around him. The passengers who are standing, mainly school children, shift their weight from one foot to the other. Those who are seated are doing their best to be invisible. A few are fanning themselves with their hands. It's hot inside and even the windows have steamed up slightly.

Next to Innocent, a thin girl wearing large gold hoop earrings exhales loudly. Lots of thin braids line her head. They're so freshly done that the tightness of each hair pinching at the scalp is visible. She reminds Innocent of his sister, Charity. The girl loops one braid round and round an index finger then sinks to her feet. She eases her bottom onto the floor of the carriage. 'Man, I'm tired,' she says. 'How much longer do we have to keep waiting?' A couple of other girls follow her example and squat down too.

'You know what I think?' Innocent raises his voice as if he's addressing a big rally. 'I think the white people should stand and let us blacks sit.'

The girls on the floor start to giggle. In the rest of the train the atmosphere becomes even flatter, like the last bubble disappearing from a fizzy drink.

Kerm can't believe what's he's hearing. He glances at Helen. 'They're crazy,' he whispers.

She puts a finger to her lips, willing him to stay silent. The last thing anyone should do in such a situation is draw attention to themselves.

'Give your seats to the niggaz!' Blessing shouts.

'Once upon a time you made us stand while you sat. It should be the other way now.' Innocent runs his eyes over the stiff figures frozen to their seats.

Kerm rises on to his tiptoes so he has a good view over the heads of the crowd. He sees what he hadn't noticed before: that by chance many of those sitting are indeed white. He also realises that more than half of the students filling the standing space are black.

'These white people,' Comfort joins in, 'they all scared of us blacks. You can tell. They go red. Jus' look. Jus' check how shook they all are.'

It's true. People *are* scared. Some of them seem to be holding their breath. Kerm can feel the fear crawling through the air. It fills him with anger. How can three teenagers have this effect on so many people? He too feels intimidated. It's crazy. 'Hey, you!' Kerm calls out. 'That's enough now.'

The boys can't see who's spoken. Innocent jumps up a couple of times, trying to work out who it might be.

'Who are you? Some smart-ass white boy? Too scared to show your face?' Innocent's nostrils flare as he breathes out sharply.

'Don't.' Helen grabs at Kerm's trousers. 'It's not worth it.'

Innocent starts to swagger through the carriage, checking everyone out. Comfort follows him. 'Come on! If you're so big, you can say it to my face. Be a man.'

Innocent grabs the tie of a spotty schoolboy whose bag happens to bump his arm. 'Was it you?' He brings his face close to the boy's.

'Leave him alone!' Kerm shouts. He's so enraged he doesn't notice the train start to move slowly. Helen tugs on his trousers again. 'You're just bullies.'

As if by some miracle leap, the two boys are suddenly standing right near Kerm.

'What's this got to do with you? Whose side are you on?' Comfort asks.

'The side of decency.'

'You got something else to say?' Innocent's jaw moves as though he's chewing gum.

'No.' Kerm's heart is pounding.

Helen looks away and hopes they don't recognise her.

'Coz, if you have, please share it.' Innocent's tone is so over-friendly it can only be read as threatening. 'No, really. You don't have to be a pussy and shout your comments while ducking behind the ladies. Tell me, bruv, I'm here to listen.' Kerm is almost a head taller than Innocent, but this doesn't seem to faze the teenager.

'I've got nothing more to say.' Kerm keeps his voice hard, his eyes locked with the boy's. He registers the metallic clack of the train in motion and hopes they pull up at the next stop soon.

'You sure?' Innocent presses closer, his chest almost touching Kerm's. 'Or you just a pussy?'

Comfort steps up so he's on one side of Kerm. 'You look like you got a problem, bruv.'

'Yes, I have a problem with your attitude. As does every other person on this train,' he adds, hoping someone else might back him up. His arms are crossed protectively over his chest, holding his coat and jacket close.

A space-y sort of buzzing noise starts, like the kind you get in science fiction movies when aliens are about to land. Helen sits bolt upright and pushes her left hand, which is holding her phone, under her thigh. Her mobile's address book is customised, giving different ringtones to people so that she can recognise the caller. The sonic sound being emitted means that Jill is calling. As part of the ringing, a nasal voice starts to croak, 'Earthlings have no fear . . .'

Innocent looks in Helen's direction and recognises her. His eyes zip back and forth between her and Kerm, trying to work out if there's a connection. Then, looking through the window behind Helen, he realises the train is moving.

'Fuck you, man.' It's a throwaway comment, a sign that he can't be bothered any more. I need to get out, he's thinking, make a run for it at the next stop. He takes a step back.

'What right do you have to speak to people like that? What have I done to you?' Kerm shouts.

Innocent has already turned away. Comfort follows, but not without stamping hard on Kerm's foot first.

'Get off me!' Kerm pushes Comfort and the back of his hand smacks him under the chin. Next thing a blow lands in Kerm's stomach. He drops his coat and jacket and hits out, punching and kicking. He hears a woman scream. The boys are cursing, hammering him with blows. He feels a sharp jab in his side and cries for help.

There's a clatter of glass breaking as someone pulls the emergency alarm. Another person calls out in relief, 'We're at the station!'

The boys charge towards an exit.

Kerm sinks to his knees, breathing heavily. He keels towards the left, clutching at his waist. His jaw is clenched, his lips pulled back, baring teeth that grind against each other in pain. Now people offer help, prop him up, express anger. Helen clambers out of her seat and crouches down next to Kerm.

She doesn't notice the bloody ball of paper fall from her hand and roll between Kerm's legs. She doesn't realise that her palm is stained a ruby red. Without thinking, she places her hand over the arm Kerm has wrapped around his wound. Her eyes are fixed on his face, so she can't see the blood leaking out of him so fast it drips onto the floor. Then she feels a warm wetness on her skin and pulls away, startled. She lifts up her hand and watches the blood run along the jagged cracks of her life and fate lines. Two fat drops roll off onto her suede coat.

THE END

Quick Reads

Books in the Quick Reads series

101 Ways to get your Child to Read	Patience Thomson
All These Lonely People	Gervase Phinn
Black-Eyed Devils	Catrin Collier
Bloody Valentine	James Patterson
Buster Fleabags	Rolf Harris
The Cave	Kate Mosse
Chickenfeed	Minette Walters
Cleanskin	Val McDermid
Clouded Vision	Linwood Barclay
A Cool Head	Ian Rankin
Danny Wallace and the Centre of the Universe	Danny Wallace
The Dare	John Boyne
Doctor Who: Code of the Krillitanes	Justin Richards
Doctor Who: I Am a Dalek	Gareth Roberts
Doctor Who: Made of Steel	Terrance Dicks
Doctor Who: Revenge of the Judoon	Terrance Dicks
Doctor Who: The Sontaran Games	Jacqueline Rayner
Dragons' Den: Your Road to Success	
A Dream Come True	Maureen Lee
Follow Me	Sheila O'Flanagan
Girl on the Platform	Josephine Cox
The Grey Man	Andy McNab
The Hardest Test	Scott Quinnell
Hell Island	Matthew Reilly

Hello Mum	Bernardine Evaristo
How to Change Your Life in 7 Steps	John Bird
Humble Pie	Gordon Ramsay
Jack and Jill	Lucy Cavendish
Kung Fu Trip	Benjamin Zephaniah
Last Night Another Soldier	Andy McNab
Life's New Hurdles	Colin Jackson
Life's Too Short	Val McDermid, Editor
Lily	Adèle Geras
Men at Work	Mike Gayle
Money Magic	Alvin Hall
My Dad's a Policeman	Cathy Glass
One Good Turn	Chris Ryan
The Perfect Holiday	Cathy Kelly
The Perfect Murder	Peter James
RaW Voices: True Stories of Hardship	Vanessa Feltz
Reaching for the Stars	Lola Jaye
Reading My Arse!	Ricky Tomlinson
Star Sullivan	Maeve Binchy
Strangers on the 16:02	Priya Basil
The Sun Book of Short Stories	
Survive the Worst and Aim for the Best	Kerry Katona
The 10 Keys to Success	John Bird
Tackling Life	Charlie Oatway
The Tannery	Sherrie Hewson
Traitors of the Tower	Alison Weir
Trouble on the Heath	Terry Jones
Twenty Tales of the War Zone	John Simpson
We Won the Lottery	Danny Buckland

Quick Reads

Great stories, great writers, great entertainment

Quick Reads are brilliantly written short new books by bestselling authors and celebrities. Whether you're an avid reader who wants a quick fix or haven't picked up a book since school, sit back, relax and let Quick Reads inspire you.

We would like to thank all our partners in the Quick Reads project for their help and support:

Arts Council England
The Department for Business, Innovation and Skills
NIACE
unionlearn
National Book Tokens
The Reading Agency
National Literacy Trust
Welsh Books Council
Basic Skills Cymru, Welsh Assembly Government
The Big Plus Scotland
DELNI
NALA

Quick Reads would also like to thank the Department for Business, Innovation and Skills; Arts Council England and World Book Day for their sponsorship and NIACE for their outreach work.

Quick Reads is a World Book Day initiative.

www.quickreads.org.uk www.worldbookday.com

Other resources

Enjoy this book? Find out about all the others from **www.quickreads.org.uk**

Free courses are available for anyone who wants to develop their skills. You can attend the courses in your local area. If you'd like to find out more, phone 0800 66 0800.

Don't get by get on 0800 66 0800

For more information on developing your basic skills in Scotland, call The Big Plus free on 0808 100 1080 or visit www.thebigplus.com

Join the Reading Agency's Six Book Challenge at www.sixbookchallenge.org.uk

Publishers Barrington Stoke (www.barringtonstoke.co.uk) and New Island (www.newisland.ie) also provide books for new readers.

The BBC runs an adult basic skills campaign. See www.bbc.co.uk/raw.

www.worldbookday.com